This book belongs to:

_____

_____

_____

To my grandsons Colton, Hunter, Kingston, Kailani and Dylan, who inspire me and whom I love with all my heart!

Colton Hunter King Kai Dylan

First Printing, 2021
Printed in the United States of America

OH NO!
MY DINOSAUR WANTS A BATH!

By J. E. Comet

Ziggy is my best friend. He is a dinosaur. We do **everything** together. Oh...and by the way, I'm James. I'm five.

This is my dinosaur Ziggy. Did I mention he's my best friend?

Mostly, Ziggy just wants to sleep, eat, play and make me laugh. He really makes me laugh!

Today Ziggy says he wants to take a bath. Where can Ziggy take a bath? Can he take a bath in the bathtub? Dinosaurs are big! I'm not sure if Ziggy will fit in the bathtub!

Ziggy **really** wants to take a bath!

I tried to fit Ziggy in
our bathtub, but just as I
thought....Ziggy is too big!
So big! Water and
bubbles got everywhere!
What a mess! Dinosaurs
do **not** fit in bathtubs.

I **have** to figure out how to get Ziggy a proper bath. After all Ziggy is my best friend and best friends help each other. How I wonder? Could Ziggy take a bath in my backyard sprinkler?

Oh no! That doesn't work! Ziggy is exhausted running around trying to get wet in the sprinkler. A dinosaur can't take a bath in a sprinkler! Ziggy is way too big!

The bathtub did not work. Ziggy is too big. The sprinklers did not work. Ziggy got too tired running around trying to get wet. But Ziggy **really** wants a bath! I wonder how I can get Ziggy a bath?

Suddenly I have an idea! My friend Sandy has a pool. Maybe Ziggy can take a bath in my friend Sandy's pool. I ask Sandy if it is alright for Ziggy to take a bath in her pool. It's important to ask someone if you can use their things. She says yes! Yay! Now Ziggy can take a bath!

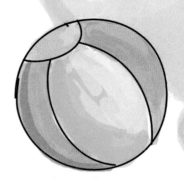

Oh no! Ziggy splashed all the water out of the pool. I guess dinosaurs shouldn't take baths in pools after all! They are just too big!

Ziggy **really wants** a bath! So, I must put on my thinking cap and come up with a way to get Ziggy his bath! There **must** be a way!

I **have** it! I finally have it! The **ocean**! I will take Ziggy to the beach so he can take a bath in the ocean. Ziggy is really **big** and the ocean is really **big**. Ziggy won't be able to make a mess in the ocean. Ziggy won't have to run around in the ocean to get wet and he can't splash all the water out of the ocean. Ziggy will be **so happy!** He will **finally** get his bath!

What a marvelous day this has been!
Ziggy wanted a bath and I figured out
a way to get Ziggy his bath! Now he is
happy and clean! Everyone should be
happy and clean. Now we can go back to
playing and sleeping and eating and
laughing.

Ziggy really makes me laugh!

.

.

Made in the USA
Coppell, TX
08 April 2023

15405099R00019